Moles Can Dance

Richard Edwards

illustrated by Caroline Anstey

Candlewick Press
Cambridge, Massachusetts

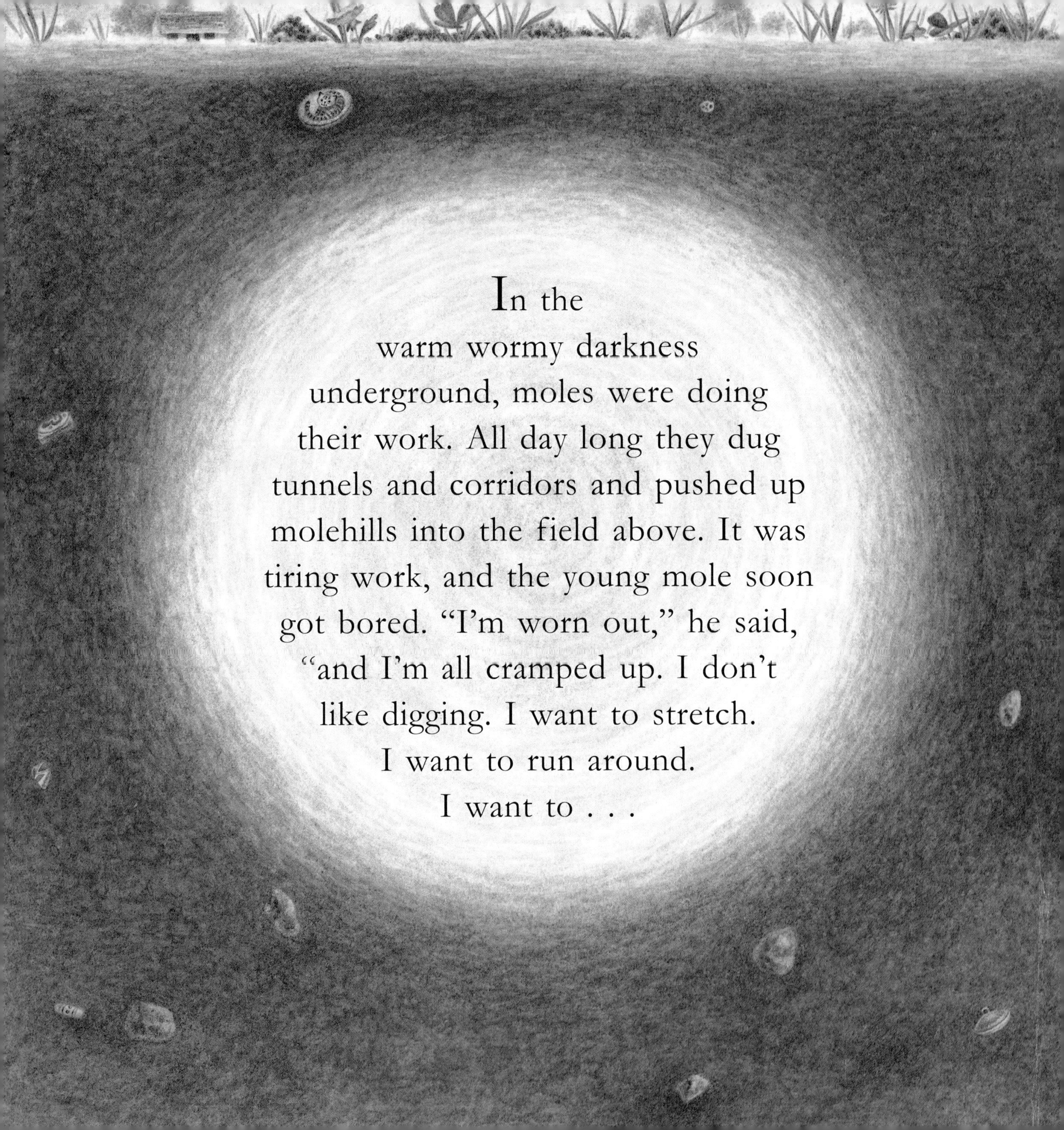

In the
warm wormy darkness
underground, moles were doing
their work. All day long they dug
tunnels and corridors and pushed up
molehills into the field above. It was
tiring work, and the young mole soon
got bored. "I'm worn out," he said,
"and I'm all cramped up. I don't
like digging. I want to stretch.
I want to run around.
I want to . . .

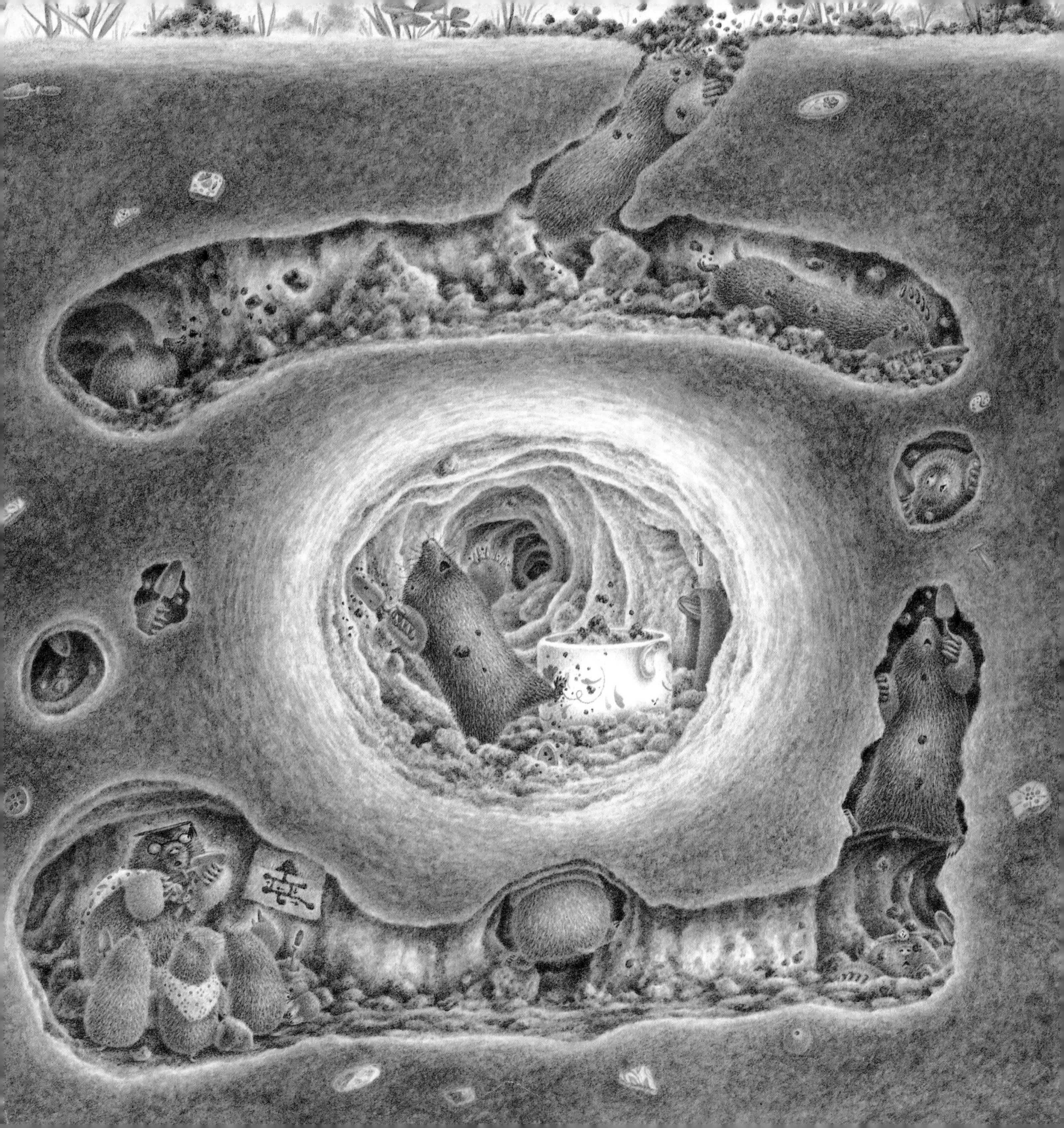

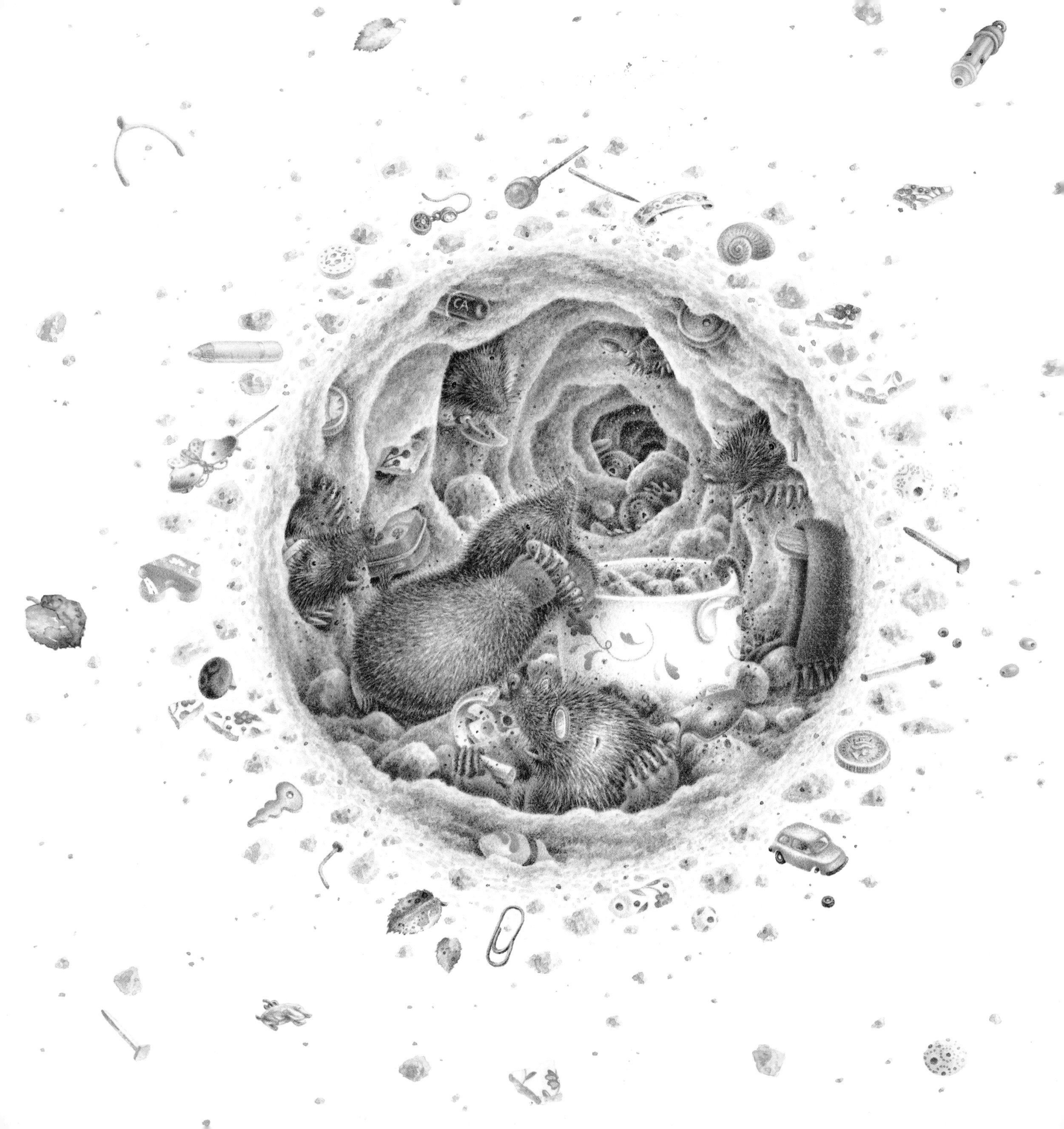

. . . *dance!*"

"Moles can't dance," said the old mole. "Moles aren't made for dancing—they're made for digging. Whoever heard of a mole dancing!"

"Moles can't dance," said all the other moles.

"See!" said the old mole. "What did I tell you? Now stop being silly and dig that tunnel."

The young mole dug as he was told, but all the time he was thinking: I want to learn to dance. Why shouldn't I learn to dance? It's not fair.

Then he had an idea. If the moles couldn't teach him to dance, maybe someone else could. Quickly he scrabbled his way upward and broke out into the dazzling sunshine of the field.

A cow was looking at him.

"I want to learn to dance," said the young mole.

"I can't teach you," said the cow. "Cows can't dance. They can chew grass and wave their tails and moo, but they can't dance."

And it went on chewing grass.

The mole walked on and met a frog.

"I want to learn to dance," said the mole.

"I can't teach you," said the frog. "Frogs can't dance. They can hop around and swim, but they can't dance."

And it hopped into the pond and swam away.

Next, the mole met a fox.
"I want to learn to dance," said the mole.
"I can't teach you," said the fox. "Foxes can't dance. They can prowl around the fields, keeping very quiet, but they can't dance."

And it went on prowling.

The mole walked on and saw a woodpecker hammering at a tree.

"I want to learn to dance," called the mole.

"I can't teach you," said the woodpecker. "Woodpeckers can't dance. They can fly from tree to tree, bashing the bark with their beaks, but they can't dance."

And it went on bashing.

Then the mole heard a funny noise coming from behind a hedge.

THUMPA THUMPA THUMPA

What could it be?

THUMPA THUMPA THUMPA

The mole crawled into the hedge and looked out on the other side. Two children were playing in a garden. Dodge was making the *THUMPA THUMPA THUMPA* by banging on some boxes, and Daisy was dancing on the grass. Real dancing!

The mole had never seen anything so fine in all his life.

Dodge drummed

and Daisy danced

and the mole watched carefully.

Daisy spun around on one leg,
and the mole spun around on one leg.

Daisy did a cartwheel,
and the mole did a cartwheel.
Daisy hopped up and down, and so did the mole.

Every step that Daisy danced,
the mole danced too, until shadows
began to creep across the garden.
"Better get back," said the mole to himself. "It's
getting late." And he turned and began
to dance his way home.

The woodpecker was
so surprised to see the mole
dancing back along the path
that it almost fell off its branch.

The fox was so surprised
to see the mole dancing
along the hedgerow
that it almost
toppled into
a ditch.

The frog was so
surprised to see the mole dancing
past the pond that it swallowed
a mouthful of muddy water.

The cow was so
surprised to see the
mole dancing across
the field that it
stood still for a long
time, with a grass
stalk sticking out
of its mouth.

"Where have you been?" asked the old mole.

"Just . . . dancing," said the young mole.

"Moles can't dance," said the old mole.

"Oh, yes they can," said the young mole. "I'll show you." And he climbed on to the top of the nearest molehill and began to hop and spin around.

Soon all the other moles came up to see what was happening.

"He's dancing!" said one mole. "And if he can, so can we.

Come on!"

So, in ones and twos and
threes, they all began to dance—
some on molehills, some on the
grass, some very badly, some very well,
some moles hopping, some moles jumping,

and some moles spinning
around, but all of them, even
the old mole, having a fine time as
they danced and danced and danced and
danced by the light of the climbing moon.